Supersonic Warrior

Supersonic Warrior

Taking Down The Darkness

Josh Zimmer

Superstar Speedsters

Dedicated to Marvel Studios and Power Rangers for inspiring the creation of Supersonic Warrior

ACKNOWLEDGEMENTS

Marvel Studios and Power Rangers- for inspiring the powers and design of Supersonic Warrior

CONTENTS

book

Justin laid in the experiment tube, with the wires connected to his body. His body was weak, from the energy that was drained during the battle with Spider Crusader and Supersonic Warrior. Justin ignited his body with flames, and heated himself up. The experiment tube shattered, as the wires disconnected from Justin's body. Justin walked out of the experiment tube, as the glass shards landed on the ground. Justin stretched his arms and legs! Justin jogged in place to energize himself. Justin walked to the cabinet, and grabbed a water bottle. Justin grabbed a towel from the table. Justin opened up the water bottle, and poured the water on to his arm. Justin wiped the blood off of his arm with the towel. Justin threw the water bottle in to the recycling bin. Justin opened up another water bottle and poured the water all over his face and body. The water washed the blood off of Justin's face and body. Justin poured some water on to his hair. Justin dried himself with the towel, and threw the water bottle in to the recycling bin. Justin put the towel on the table, and walked toward the debris on the floor. Justin walked through the debris, from the chaos that happened during the battle. Justin rubbed his head and said, "That was a rough battle." Justin looked around the room for a window, that he can jump through, since Supersonic Warrior is probably causing chaos in the city. Justin walked to the other side of the room, and saw a window. Justin smashed the window open with a fire blast. Justin climbed out of the window, and ignited his body with flames to protect himself. Justin landed on the ground, while the birds tweeted in the background. Justin saw the glider in the air, and noticed that he isn't far from Supersonic Warrior's location. Justin walked down the sidewalk, and cars were zooming down the street. Police cars zoomed past Justin, with their sirens on. Justin walked further down the sidewalk, and noticed the gasoline station in front of him. Justin noticed that the glider was parked at the gasoline station. Justin hid behind the pole, and looked inside the window. The gasoline store was filled with drinks and snacks that can be bought at the register. Supersonic Warrior was in the gasoline station, threatening the cashier. Supersonic Warrior growled and said, "Give me all of your money, human scum, or you will die." Daniel trembled in fear and said, "I don't have much money in the cash register, and the gas station will collapse without it." Supersonic Warrior's shadow tendrils grabbed Daniel by the neck, and smashed him through the counter. Daniel laid on the ground! Supersonic Warrior said, "Don't make me angry, or you will regret it." Supersonic Warrior stepped on Daniel's chest, and her shadow tendrils wrapped around Daniel's neck. Supersonic Warrior summoned a ice shard in to her hand, with her ice blast. Supersonic Warrior's shadow tendrils lifted Daniel in to the air. Supersonic Warrior stabbed the ice shard in to Daniel's chest. Supersonic Warrior's shadow tendrils threw Daniel in to the wall. Daniel laid on the ground, in a puddle of blood. Supersonic Warrior ignited a dark blast from her body. Everything in the gas station exploded! Glass shards and wood pieces landed on the ground. Supersonic Warrior walked through the debris. Justin jumped through the broken window, and pointed his fire gauntlet at Supersonic Warrior. Justin shot a fire blast at Supersonic Warrior. Supersonic Warrior dodged the fire blast, and shot her shadow tendrils at Justin. Justin shot fire blasts at the shadow tendrils. The shadow tendrils burnt to a crisp. Supersonic Warrior growled, and regenerated her shadow tendrils. Supersonic Warrior shot the shadow tendrils at Justin. The shadow tendrils wrapped around Justin. Supersonic Warrior said, "The little pest tried to pounce on the predator." Supersonic Warrior rubbed her hand in Justin's hair. Justin whacked Supersonic Warrior's hand away. Justin said, "I will stop you, because I am a hero!" Supersonic

Warrior said, "Heroes are worthless scum, despair will take over the world!" Supersonic Warrior's shadow tendrils smashed Justin in to the wall. Justin growled and lit up his arm with flames. Justin touched one of the shadow tendrils, and lit it on fire. Supersonic Warrior screamed in pain, as the shadow goop landed on the ground. Justin smiled and said, "Here's my chance to strike back!" Justin shot a fire grenade at Supersonic Warrior. Supersonic Warrior smashed in to the wall. Justin ignited a fire blast from his body. Supersonic Warrior smashed through the wall, and laid on the ground. Supersonic Warrior growled, as she got up from the ground. Justin backflipped in the air, and shot a fire missile from his gauntlet at Supersonic Warrior. Supersonic Warrior smashed through the wall, as shadow goop fell on the ground. Supersonic Warrior laid on the ground! Justin ignited a fire blast from his body. Everything exploded around Justin, as it fell on the ground. Supersonic Warrior got up from the ground, and growled at Justin. Supersonic Warrior said, "You caused me pain and suffering." Supersonic Warrior's shadow tendrils grabbed Justin, and smashed him in to the ground, multiple times. Justin growled, as he lit his body on fire. The shadow tendrils lit on fire, and lost their grip on Justin. Justin roundhouse kicked Supersonic Warrior in the chest. Supersonic Warrior smashed through the counter, and laid next to the wall. Justin walked toward Supersonic Warrior! Justin smiled, as his eyes glowed red. Justin stood in front of Supersonic Warrior and said, "I have figured out your weakness, how does it feel to be another ordinary villain, consumed by darkness?" Supersonic Warrior said, "You can't stop me, I will fill your mind with despair." Justin lit his arm with flames, and picked up Supersonic Warrior by the neck. Justin said, "Despair will not win!" Supersonic Warrior's suit lit on fire, as she growled in pain. The shadow tendrils are weakening, as the flames burnt them. Supersonic Warrior's suit is burnt to a crisp. Justin smashed Supersonic Warrior in to the ground. Supersonic Warrior laid on the ground! Justin punched Supersonic Warrior in the face with a fire blast. Supersonic Warrior's visor shattered, as she laid on the ground. Supersonic Warrior's suit repaired itself, as the shadow goop reconnected to her suit. The visor repaired itself, and Supersonic Warrior got up from the ground. Supersonic Warrior growled, and ignited a shadow explosion from her body. Justin rolled on the ground, and smashed in to the wall. Justin laid against the wall! Justin backflipped off of the ground. Justin loaded a grenade in to his gauntlet, and shot it at Supersonic Warrior. The grenade hit Supersonic Warrior in the chest. Supersonic Warrior slid backwards, as shadow goop fell on to the ground. Supersonic Warrior growled, and sped toward Justin. Supersonic Warrior shot her shadow tendrils at Justin. The shadow tendrils wrapped around Justin's body. Supersonic Warrior smashed Justin in to the ground. Supersonic Warrior pulled Justin in to the air, and threw him in to the wall. Justin laid against the wall. Supersonic Warrior said, "Thanks for the little distraction, human scum." Supersonic Warrior walked to the glider. Supersonic Warrior walked on to the glider, and flew in to the air. Justin got up from the ground, and rubbed his head. Justin walked further down the street. Justin saw the glider hovering over the area, as Supersonic Warrior's shadow tendrils stabbed the citizens in the chest, and killed them. The dead bodies of the citizens laid on the ground, as Justin followed the glider. Supersonic Warrior's shadow tendrils tore the fire hydrants out of the ground, and threw them in to the wall. The water from the fire hydrants poured in to the city. The fire hydrants were spraying water everywhere. Justin walked further down the sidewalk, and got soaked by the fire hydrants. The water dripped off of Justin's body, as he ran after the glider. Citizens were panicking and running away from Supersonic Warrior, as the glider hovered down the sidewalk. Supersonic Warrior shot web bombs from the glider at the buildings. The buildings crumbled, and smashed the panicking citizens on to the ground. Dead bodies laid on the sidewalk in puddles of blood. Justin was jumping over the dead bodies, as he chased the glider down the sidewalk. Justin flipped in to the air, and shot a fire blast from his gauntlet at the glider. The glider spun in to the building, and smashed through one of the citizens. The citizen laid on the sidewalk in a puddle of blood. Justin jumped over the dead body, as Supersonic Warrior regained her balance on the glider. The glider hovered further down the sidewalk. Justin ran after the glider! Panicking citizens were running away from Supersonic Warrior's glider. Supersonic Warrior's shadow tendrils were stabbing various citizens in the chest, as their bodies laid on the ground. Supersonic Warrior's shadow tendrils picked up several cars, and threw them at Justin. Justin backflipped over the cars, and dodged them. Justin swung on a tree branch, and backflipped in to the tree. Justin shot a fire grenade from his gauntlet at the glider. The glider spun in to a building and crashed. Supersonic warrior laid on the glider. Justin backflipped out of the tree, and on to the glider. Justin punched Supersonic Warrior in the chest with a fire blast. Supersonic Warrior growled in pain! Supersonic Warrior shot a shadow tendril at Justin's neck. The shadow tendril wrapped around Justin's neck. Supersonic Warrior smashed Justin in to the wall, multiple times, and threw him in to the pole. Justin smashed in to the pole, and laid on the ground. The pole fell over, and landed on the ground. Supersonic Warrior got up, and reattached herself to the glider. The glider hovered down the sidewalk. Justin got up from the ground. Justin ran further down the sidewalk, and chased the glider. Supersonic Warrior's shadow tendrils threw shadow bombs at Justin. Justin flipped in the air, and shot the shadow bombs out of the air with fire blasts. Justin shot a fire grenade at Supersonic Warrior's glider. The fire grenade exploded one of the shadow tendrils in to shadow goop. Supersonic Warrior growled, as the shadow tendril regenerated. Supersonic Warrior hovered the glider toward Oasis Falls High School. Justin followed behind Supersonic Warrior. Oasis Falls High School was in Supersonic Warrior's view. Supersonic Warrior parked the glider next to the flag pole. Supersonic Warrior detached from the glider, and walked off of the glider. Justin backflipped over the glider, and roundhouse kicked Supersonic Warrior in the chest. Supersonic Warrior slid backwards! Supersonic Warrior tore the flag pole out of the ground, and hit Justin in the chest. Justin rolled on the ground! Justin backflipped off of the ground. Supersonic Warrior shot her shadow tendrils at Justin. Justin backflipped over them, and shot a fire grenade at Supersonic Warrior. Supersonic Warrior smashed in to a tree and growled. Supersonic Warrior laid against the tree. Justin sped toward Supersonic Warrior! Justin lit his arm with flames, and grabbed Supersonic Warrior by the neck. Justin smashed Supersonic Warrior in to the ground, as the shadow goop on her suit burnt in to a crisp. The shadow goop fell off of Supersonic Warrior's suit, and landed on the ground. Supersonic Warrior growled, and ignited a shadow explosion from her body. Justin smashed in to the tree, and got stuck to the tree by a shadow goop web. Justin ignited his body in flames, and burned the shadow goop web off of him. Justin back-flipped and roundhouse kicked Supersonic Warrior in the face. Supersonic Warrior slid backwards, and shot shadow tendrils at Justin. Justin backflipped and dodged the shadow tendrils. Justin shot a fire blast at Supersonic Warrior. Supersonic Warrior smashed in to the tree, and laid on the ground. Supersonic Warrior got up from the ground. Justin ran toward Supersonic Warrior, and flipped in to a tree. Justin swung on the tree branch, and flipped in to the air. Justin summoned a fire aura around his body, and spun in to a tornado. Justin spun in to Supersonic Warrior! The shadow goop burnt off of Supersonic Warrior's suit, and fell on the ground. Supersonic Warrior smashed in to the wall, and laid on the ground. Justin landed on the ground, as the fire aura disappeared around his body. Justin backflipped on to Supersonic Warrior, and held her on the ground. Justin ignited his arm with flames, and put his hand on Supersonic Warrior's chest. The shadow goop started to burn, as Supersonic Warrior growled. Supersonic Warrior shot a shadow tendril at Justin, Justin grabbed the shadow tendril, and burnt it to a crisp. The shadow goop fell on to the ground. Supersonic Warrior growled, and tossed Justin off of her. Justin rolled on the ground. Supersonic Warrior got up from the ground. Justin got up from the ground. Justin shot a fire blast at Supersonic Warrior. Supersonic Warrior smashed in to a tree, and laid on the ground. Supersonic Warrior growled, as she backflipped off of the ground! Justin said, "Hey shadow demon, come chase me through the school!" Justin shot a fire grenade at Supersonic

Warrior. The fire grenade hit Supersonic Warrior's chest, and exploded. The shadow goop fell off of her suit, and on to the ground. Supersonic Warrior growled, as the shadow goop regenerated. Justin kicked open the doors for Oasis Falls High School. Justin ran in to Oasis Falls High School. Supersonic Warrior chased after Justin. Supersonic Warrior picked up lockers with her shadow tendrils, and threw them at Justin. Justin backflipped in to the air, and dodged them. The lockers fell on to the ground, as Justin ran further down the hallway. Supersonic Warrior chased after Justin! Justin shot a fire blast at Supersonic Warrior. The fire blast hit Supersonic Warrior in the chest! Supersonic Warrior slid backwards and growled, as the shadow goop fell off of her suit. Justin ran to the water fountain, while Supersonic Warrior was chasing him. Justin stopped at the water fountain, and picked it up. Justin threw the water fountain at Supersonic Warrior. The water fountain splashed water all over Supersonic Warrior. Supersonic Warrior slid backwards! Supersonic Warrior growled, and shot a shadow tendril at Justin. The shadow tendril wrapped around Justin, and smashed him in to the lockers. Justin laid against the lockers. Supersonic Warrior walked toward Justin, and growled at him. Justin shot a fire grenade at Supersonic Warrior. Supersonic Warrior slid backwards, and Justin got up from the ground. Justin ran in to the science lab. Supersonic Warrior chased after Justin! Justin ran toward the science cabinet, and threw containers of chemicals at Supersonic Warrior. The chemicals splashed on to the shadow goop, and dissolved it. The shadow goop fell off of Supersonic Warrior's suit, as she growled in pain. Supersonic Warrior tackled Justin in to the chemical table. The chemicals splashed on top of Supersonic Warrior's suit. Supersonic Warrior growled, as she held Justin on the ground. Supersonic Warrior's visor glowed red, as she stared in to Justin's eyes. Justin growled and punched Supersonic Warrior in the chest, with a fire blast. Supersonic Warrior rolled on to the ground. Justin got up from the ground. Supersonic Warrior got up from the ground! Supersonic Warrior sped toward Justin! Supersonic Warrior ignited a shadow blast from her body. The furniture and the chemical tubes exploded, and fell on the ground. Justin smashed in to the desk, and laid next to it. Supersonic Warrior walked toward Justin, with her red visor glowing. Supersonic Warrior grabbed Justin by his neck, and threw him in to the teacher's desk. Justin smashed through the teacher's desk. Justin got up from the ground, and threw the left over pieces of the teacher's desk at Supersonic Warrior. Supersonic Warrior slid backwards, and growled. Justin tackled Supersonic Warrior through the science lab door, and in to the hallway lockers. Supersonic Warrior laid against the lockers. Justin punched Supersonic Warrior in the chest, with a fire blast. Supersonic Warrior laid on the ground. Justin held Supersonic Warrior on the ground! Justin punched Supersonic Warrior in the face, multiple times. Supersonic Warrior's visor started to crack. Supersonic Warrior growled, and shot a shadow laser from her visor at Justin. Justin rolled on the ground! Supersonic Warrior's visor repaired itself, while she got up from the ground. Justin got up from the ground. Justin shot a fire blast at Supersonic Warrior. The fire blast hit Supersonic Warrior's chest. Supersonic Warrior slid backwards, as shadow goop fell off of her suit. Supersonic Warrior growled, as she grabbed a book shelf with her shadow tendrils. Supersonic Warrior threw the book shelf at Justin. Justin caught the book shelf, as he slid backwards. Justin threw the book shelf at Supersonic Warrior. Supersonic Warrior smashed in to the wall. Supersonic Warrior got up from the ground. Supersonic Warrior growled, and chased after Justin. Justin ran in to the library, and flipped on to the book shelf. Justin balanced himself on the book shelf. Supersonic Warrior growled, as Justin kicked the books off of the book shelf at her. Supersonic Warrior exploded the books to pieces with her shadow blast. Justin kicked the book shelf down on top of Supersonic Warrior, as he flipped on to the next book shelf. Supersonic Warrior smashed the book shelf to pieces with her shadow blast. Justin backflipped off of the book shelf. Justin ignited a fire blast from his body! Everything in the library exploded, and fell on top of Supersonic Warrior. Supersonic Warrior growled, as she got up from the ground. Justin tackled Supersonic Warrior, and body slammed her in to the ground. Justin ignited his arm with flames, as he put his arm on Supersonic warrior's neck. Supersonic Warrior growled in pain, as the flames burnt her suit. Supersonic Warrior shot a shadow laser from her visor at Justin. Justin rolled on the ground. Supersonic warrior got up from the ground. Justin got up from the ground. Justin ran out of the library, and Supersonic Warrior chased after him. Justin ran in to the biology lab. Supersonic warrior growled at Justin. Justin saw the piranha tank, and smiled. Justin ran to the closet in the biology lab, and put on a piranha resistant armor suit. Justin said,"Time for a little swim for you, monster!" Justin stood in front of the piranha tank. Supersonic Warrior ran toward Justin! Justin ignited his arm with flames, and punched Supersonic Warrior in to the air." Justin flipped in the air, and kicked Supersonic Warrior in to the piranha tank. Supersonic Warrior grabbed on to Justin's leg, and pulled him in to the piranha tank with her. Supersonic Warrior and Justin landed in the piranha tank. The piranha fish swam around Justin and Supersonic Warrior, as they floated in the tank. The piranha fish attached to Supersonic Warrior, as she growled in pain. Justin ignited a fire blast from his body. The water heated up, and spun in to a tornado. The shadow goop was boiled off of Supersonic Warrior's suit. Supersonic Warrior was floating in the water, as the piranha fish tore her suit to pieces. Justin swam to the top of the piranha tank. Justin got to the top of the piranha tank, and climbed out of it. Justin landed on the ground! The piranha tank closed, as the piranha fish tore up its prey. The piranha fish summoned a tornado in the tank, as the bubbles in the water started forming together. Supersonic Warrior's suit was torn apart, with her helmet destroyed, and her visor has been shattered. The water turned red, as the blood from Supersonic Warrior's suit soaked through it. The piranha tank opened, and the piranha fish swam in their group. Supersonic Warrior's body laid at the bottom of the tank. Justin grabbed a fishing net, and fished Supersonic Warrior out of the tank. Justin laid Supersonic Warrior on the ground! A glider smashed through the window, and landed in front of Justin. Spider Crusader walked off of the glider, and growled at Justin. Justin pointed his fire gauntlet at Spider Crusader, and loaded a fire grenade in to it. Justin shot the fire grenade at Spider Crusader! The fire grenade hit Spider Crusader in the chest. Spider Crusader slid backwards!Spider Crusader said, "Human scum, prepare to die!" Justin said, "I will defend this city from you, monster!" Spider Crusader said, "I will smash you like a bug, hero." Spider Crusader smiled, as he took out his web sword. Justin said, "You will fail, like every other villain." Justin backflipped in the air, and kicked Spider Crusader in the chest. Spider Crusader smashed in to the wall! Spider Crusader laid against the wall, and growled. Spider Crusader shot a web in Justin's face, and grabbed him by the neck. Spider crusader smashed Justin in to the ground. Justin shot a fire blast at Spider Crusader. Spider Crusader smashed through the wall, and laid on the ground. Spider Crusader backflipped off of the ground. Justin backflipped off of the ground. Justin summoned a flaming sword in to his hand, and sped toward Spider Crusader. Spider Crusader sped toward Justin! Justin and Spider Crusader clashed their swords together, and growled at each other. Justin flipped in the air, and slashed Spider Crusader's arm with his sword. Spider Crusader slid backwards! Spider Crusader shot a web at Justin. The web attached to Justin's body. Spider Crusader pulled on the web, and dragged Justin toward him. Justin backflipped in the air, and stabbed his sword in to Spider Crusader's chest. Spider Crusader slid backwards, and growled. Spider Crusader sped in to Justin, and grabbed him by the neck. Spider Crusader smashed Justin in to the wall. Justin's sword fell on to the ground, and fizzled away. Justin laid against the wall. Justin kicked Spider Crusader in the chest. Spider Crusader slid backwards, and his web sword landed on the ground. Spider Crusader webbed his web sword back to his belt. Justin tackled Spider Crusader, and smashed him in to the ground. Justin lit up his arm with flames, and grabbed Spider Crusader by the neck. Justin lifted Spider Crusader in to the air, and threw him in to the wall. Spider Crusader laid against the wall. Justin punched Spider Crusader in the face, with a fire blast. Spider Crusader laid on the ground! Justin growled and punched Spider Crusader in the face, multiple times. Spider Crusader held Justin's arm back, and kicked him in the chest. Justin slid backwards, and Spider Crusader backflipped off of the ground. Spider Crusader threw a web bomb at Justin. The web bomb exploded, and Justin smashed in to the wall. Justin laid on the ground. Spider Crusader walked toward Justin, and growled at him. Spider Crusader stepped on Justin's chest, and held him on the ground. Spider Crusader shot electric webs at Justin. The electric webs electrocuted Justin, as blood leaked on to the ground. Spider Crusader punched Justin in the face, multiple times. Justin growled, as he lit his arm with flames. Justin held Spider Crusader's arm back. Spider Crusader's arm lit on fire. Justin backflipped off of the ground, and kicked Spider Crusader in the chest. Spider Crusader slid backwards! Spider Crusader's arm healed, as he shot webs at Justin. The webs attached to Justin's body. Spider Crusader pulled Justin toward him! Spider Crusader kicked Justin in the chest. Justin slid backwards! Spider Crusader sped in to Justin, and grabbed him by his neck. Spider Crusader smashed Justin in to the wall. Justin laid against the wall, and ignited a fire blast from his body. Spider Crusader slid backwards. Justin threw a fire grenade at Spider Crusader. Spider Crusader smashed in to the wall. Spider Crusader laid against the wall. Justin walked toward Spider Crusader, with his eyes glowing red. Justin lit his arms with flames, and picked up Spider Crusader's body. Justin smashed Spider Crusader in to the ground. Justin said, "You're a monster for the damage that you have caused to the city." Justin held Spider Crusader on the ground. Justin put his hand on Spider Crusader's chest. Spider Crusader's suit started to heat up. Spider Crusader growled, and shot a web in Justin's face. Justin slid backwards! Spider Crusader backflipped off of the ground. Spider Crusader threw some sticky web bombs on to the walls. The sticky web bombs attached to the walls, and lit up. Spider Crusader backflipped in the air, and shot webs at Justin. The webs wrapped Justin in to a cocoon. Spider Crusader sped in to the web cocoon, and kicked it in to the wall. The cocoon bounced off of the walls! The cocoon smashed on the ground, and exploded. Justin laid on the ground. Justin got up from the ground. Spider Crusader crawled on the walls. Spider Crusader crawled to the light post, above Justin. Spider Crusader shot a web from his web shooter on to the light post, and hung upside down on it. Justin stepped backwards, and pointed his fire gauntlet at Spider Crusader. Justin shot a fire grenade at Spider Crusader. Spider Crusader swung himself on the light post, and flipped in to the air. Spider Crusader shot a web at the fire grenade, and swung it toward Justin. The fire grenade hit Justin in the chest. Justin smashed in to the wall, and laid next to it. Spider Crusader landed on the ground, and pressed a button on his wrist. The glider flew in to the building. Spider crusader backflipped on to the glider, and flew around the room. Spider Crusader attached web bombs to the wall foundation. Justin got up from the ground. Spider Crusader shot a web missile from his glider at the light post. The light post exploded, and fell on to the ground. Justin flipped out of the way, as the light post smashed on to the ground in pieces. Justin loaded a fire grenade in to his fire gauntlet. Justin shot the fire grenade at Spider Crusader's glider. The fire grenade hit the glider! The glider spun in a circle, while Spider Crusader kept his balance. Spider Crusader pressed the button on his wrist, and the web bombs beeped! The web bombs exploded and the wall foundation crumbled to pieces. The wall foundation fell on top of Justin, as he got smashed on to the ground. Spider Crusader flew out of the building. Justin laid under the crumbled wall foundation, in a puddle of blood. Justin used his strength to lift the crumbled wall foundation off of him. Justin threw the crumbled wall foundation to the other side of the room. Justin sat on the ground to catch his breath. Justin wiped the blood off of his body, with a towel. Justin drank a bottle of water to rehydrate himself. Justin got up from the ground, and walked through the crumbled wall foundation. Justin walked to the window, and shattered it open with a fire blast. Justin climbed out of the window. Justin landed on the ground. Justin walked down the sidewalk, and the birds were buzzing in the background. The clouds turned gray, and it started to rain. The rain poured from the clouds, on top of Justin's body. Justin's hair was soaked, while he was walking. The glider flew in the air, while Justin was walking in the rain. Justin walked past Electric Industries. Electric Industries was empty, with no guards patrolling the area. Justin sighed, as he walked further down the sidewalk. The glider flew in to one of the windows of Electric Industries and smashed through it. Spider Crusader backflipped off of the glider, and walked through the science lab. Spider Crusader pressed a button on his wrist, and walked through the secret door. Spider Crusader walked through the secret hallway, in to a giant science lab. The giant science lab was filled with experiment tubes, and other gadgets. Spider Crusader walked to the computer, and plugged in his flash drive. Spider Crusader tapped some buttons, and loaded up the storage for the flash drive. Spider Crusader tapped on the Extreme virus, and loaded it on to the screen. Spider Crusader browsed through the data, and growled at himself. Spider Crusader said, "I thought my calculations were right when creating the virus, but the hero scum, Justin, found a weakness in my data." Spider Crusader scrolled through the data! Spider Crusader said, "The Extreme virus enhances the abilities of the host. If I change some values in the data, maybe the virus can defeat anything in its path." Spider Crusader edited the data for the Extreme virus, and made some enhancements to make it stronger. Spider Crusader smiled and said, "We just need another host for the virus to control." Spider Crusader pressed the save button on the computer, and saved the data to the flash drive. Spider Crusader spun in his chair and said, "This is why I am the smartest villain in the world, I can reconfigure any plan to outsmart my enemies." Justin walked further down the sidewalk! The rain poured harder on top of Justin, as he walked down the sidewalk. The rain was dripping off of Justin's body, as he walked down the sidewalk. Justin saw the gym in the distance, and smiled. Justin said, "The gym looks like a good place to dry for a while." Justin walked to the gym. Justin walked in to the gym, and shook the water off of his body. Justin dried his hair with a towel. Justin walked to the treadmill, and turned it on. Justin ran on the treadmill! Justin turned off the treadmill, and walked off of it. Justin walked to the workout machine, and worked out for 30 minutes. Justin walked away from the workout machine. Justin walked to the punching bag, and punched the bag for 30 minutes. Justin walked away from the punching bag, and drank a bottle of water to rehydrate himself. Justin recycled the bottle of water in the recycling bin. Justin stretched his arms and smiled. Justin said, "That was a good workout session." Justin walked to the snack vending machine in the gym. Justin paid for a ice cream bar. Justin grabbed the ice cream bar out of the snack vending machine. Justin grabbed a napkin from the counter! Justin walked to the bench! Justin sat on the bench, and ate the ice cream bar. Justin wiped his mouth with the napkin. Justin got up from the bench! Justin walked to the trash can! Justin threw the ice cream bar wrapper, and the napkin in to the trash can. Justin walked out of the gym. Justin walked down the sidewalk. Justin walked to a dark alley, and noticed a robber and a girl. The robber was dressed in black, and had a knife in his hand. The girl's name was Ash! Justin walked in to the dark alley. The robber threatened Ash with the knife. The robber said, "Hello little girl, your hair is so soft. Do you mind if I cut it off?" The robber rubbed his knife through Ash's hair. Ash was terrified in fear, and shoved the robber away from her. The robber said, "The little girl is fighting back! Time to crush your soul to pieces!" The robber smiled, as he flipped his knife in to the air. The robber backflipped and caught the knife. The robber landed on the ground. The robber kicked Ash in the back. Ash smashed in to the wall, and laid next to it. The robber slashed his knife through Ash's hair and cut it to pieces. Hair pieces landed on the ground, as Ash screamed and stumbled backwards in to the wall! The robber grabbed Ash by the neck, and stabbed his knife in to Ash's skull. Blood splashed on to the ground, as the robber threw Ash's body on to the ground. Justin walked toward the robber, as he loaded a grenade in to his gauntlet. Justin pointed the gauntlet at the robber, and pulled the trigger. The grenade hit the robber in the chest, and exploded. The robber smashed in to the wall, and laid next to it. Justin sped in to the robber, and grabbed him by the neck. Justin smashed the robber in to the ground. Justin held the robber on the ground, and punched him in the face, multiple times. Blood leaked from the robber's face, on to the ground. Justin lit his arm on fire, and put his hand on the robber's neck. The robber's body lit on fire, as blood poured out of it. The blood soaked through the robber's body, and formed a puddle. Justin got up from the ground, and wiped the blood off of his arm with a towel. Justin walked out of the alley! Justin walked down the sidewalk, and listened to the birds in the background. Justin walked to his house. Justin stopped at the front door of his house, and sighed to himself. Justin's house was blue, and has a descent sized yard for plants and playing outside. Justin took his key out of his pocket, and put it in to the door knob. Justin turned the key, and the door unlocked. Justin opened the door and walked in to the house. Justin put his bag on the rack, next to the door. Justin took his shoes off, and put them next to the rack. Justin walked to the couch, and sat on it. Justin watched football on the television. Justin's parents, Aaron and Sunshine, walked in to the room, and sat on the couch. Aaron and Sunshine sat next to Justin. Justin's eyes were watering, as he thought of Christina in his head. Aaron said, "Just let the tears out, everything will be ok." Justin broke in to tears, and cried in Sunshine's arms. Aaron rubbed Justin's back, as he cried. Sunshine said, "I know it is hard to lose one of your friends, but life will get better." Aaron and Sunshine hugged Justin, as he cried his tears out. Justin lifted his head out of Sunshine's arms, and wiped his tears away with his hands. Justin hugged Aaron and Sunshine. Justin said, "Thanks for making me feel better!" Aaron and Sunshine smiled at Justin and said, "You're welcome!" Justin turned off the television, and got up from the couch. Aaron and Sunshine got up from the couch, and walked out of the room. Justin walked out of the room, and in to the hallway. Justin walked down the hallway to his room. Justin stopped at the door, and turned the door knob. Justin opened the door, and walked in to his room. Justin laid on the bed, and went under the bed sheets. Justin closed his eyes, and fell asleep! Justin had a nightmare! In the nightmare sequence, Justin was in the woods, admiring the water fall. A pack of wolves pounced on Justin. Justin fell in to the water, as the wolves held him down. Justin ignited a fire blast from his body. The wolves got blasted further in to the woods. Justin got up from the water, and bent down. Justin looked in the water, and saw a reflection of Spider Crusader. Spider Crusader's reflection said, "You are worthless and weak, you don't deserve to be a hero." Justin whacked the water with his hand, and the reflection disappeared. Justin said, "I am a hero, and you can't tear me down!" Justin woke up from the nightmare sequence, and took the bed sheets off of his head. Justin laid on his bed, and drank a bottle of water. Justin threw the bottle in to the recycling bin, that was in his room. Justin made his bed, and straighten out the bed sheets. Sunshine knocked on the door of Justin's bed room. Justin said, "Come in!" Sunshine opened the door, and walked in to Justin's bed room. Sunshine said, "Do you want a snack from the kitchen?" Justin said, "Sure!" Justin got up from his bed, and walked to the door. Sunshine walked behind Justin, and closed the door. Justin and Sunshine walked to the kitchen. Justin and Sunshine walked in to the kitchen. Justin went to the cabinet and grabbed a bag of potato chips, and a bowl. Justin poured the bag of potato chips in to the bowl. Justin put the bag of potato chips in to the cabinet, and closed it. Justin sat at the table, and slowly ate the potato chips in the bowl. Aaron was at the table, across from Justin, eating a salad. Aaron said, "I had a friend in the past. His name was Matt!" Justin said, "What happened to Matt?" Aaron said, "Matt and I were at the aquarium, and there was a display with a huge piranha tank. Matt wanted to be confident, and swim with the piranha fish, without the security guards noticing him." Justin said, "Did he get to swim with the piranha fish?" Aaron said, "Nope, the piranha fish got mad at him and tore his body to shreds in front of me." Justin broke in to tears, and cried in his bowl of potato chips. Sunshine hit Aaron in the back, with her hand. Sunshine said, "That story was uncalled for! It wouldn't make Justin feel better!" Aaron said, "I was trying to cheer him up!" Sunshine said, "You should of tried harder!" Justin wiped his tears away with his hand and said, "Stop fighting, family members aren't allowed to fight!" Sunshine said, "Justin is right, we shouldn't fight over silly things!" Aaron and Sunshine apologize to each other, while Justin finished his bowl of potato chips. Justin got up from the table, and pushed his chair in. Justin put the empty bowl in to the dish washer. Justin closed the dishwasher! Justin walked out of the kitchen, and in to the hallway. Justin walked to the workout room. Justin walked to the door, and turned the door knob. Justin opened the door, and walked in to the workout room. Justin did push ups on the ground for 30 minutes. Justin got up from the ground, and climbed on the rock wall for 30 minutes. Justin got off of the rock wall, and took a small break. Justin drank a bottle of water to rehydrate himself. Justin threw the bottle of water in to the recycling bin. Justin walked to the workout machine. Justin worked out on the workout machine for 30 minutes. Justin walked off the workout machine, and walked to the punching bag. Justin punched the punching bag for 30 minutes. Justin walked away from the punching bag. Justin drank another bottle of water to rehydrate himself! Justin threw the water bottle in to the recycling bin. Justin stretched his arms, as he walked out of the workout room. Justin walked down the hallway! Justin walked toward the bathroom. Justin walked to the bathroom door. Justin turned the door knob, and opened the door. Justin walked in to the bathroom, and locked the door behind him. Justin turned on the water in the shower, and took off his clothes. The water warmed up in the shower. Justin walked in to the shower, and closed the shower door. Justin squirted soap out of the bottle on to his hair. Justin rubbed the soap in to his hair, with his hands. Justin washed the soap out of his hair. Justin squirted soap on to his arms. Justin washed the soap off of his arms. Justin stood under the shower head, and let the water pour on to his body. The water washed the dirt off of Justin's body. Justin turned off the water, and opened the shower door. Justin put the towel on his head, and dried off his hair. Justin wrapped the towel around his body, and dried himself. Justin put his clothes back on! Justin walked in to the hallway. Justin walked to his bed room. Justin opened the door, and walked in to his bed room. Justin walked to the bed. Justin laid on the bed. Justin sighed to himself! It was a crazy day for Justin. Justin was glad, that he can lay in bed in the comfort of his house. The sun was setting outside his bed room. The sky turned black, and the moon rose in to the sky. Justin laid under the bed sheets, and fell asleep. Justin slept for multiple hours. The sun rose in the sky, and shined through Justin's bed room window. Justin woke up, and removed the bed sheets off of his head. Justin laid on his bed, and stretched his arms. Justin got up from his bed, and jogged in place to energize himself. Justin drank a bottle of water to hydrate himself. Justin threw the bottle of water in to the recycling bin. Justin walked toward the door. Justin turned the door knob, and opened the door. Justin walked out of his room, and in to the hallway. Justin walked toward the workout room. Justin walked in to the workout room. Justin walked on to the treadmill, and ran on it for 30 minutes. Justin walked to the workout machine, and worked out on it for 30 minutes. Justin walked to the punching bag, and punched it for 30 minutes. Justin drank a bottle of water to hydrate himself. Justin threw the bottle of water in to the recycling bin. Justin walked out of the workout room, and in to the hallway. Justin walked to the bathroom. Justin walked in to the bathroom, and locked the door. Justin turned on the water in the shower, and took off his clothes. The water warmed up in the shower. Justin walked in to the shower, and closed the shower door. Justin squirted soap out of the bottle on to his hair. Justin rubbed the soap in to his hair, with his hands. Justin washed the soap out of his hair. Justin squirted soap on to his arms. Justin washed the soap off of his arms. Justin stood under the shower head, and let the water pour on to his body. The water washed the dirt off of Justin's body. Justin turned off the water, and opened the shower door. Justin put the towel on his head, and dried off his hair. Justin wrapped the towel around his body, and dried himself. Justin put his clothes back on! Justin walked in to the hallway. Justin walked to the front door! Justin stood in front of the front door, and turned the door knob. Justin walked out of the front door. Justin walked to the swing on the front porch, and sat on it. Justin swung on the swing, and listened to the birds tweeting in the background. Butterflies were flying around the flowers, while Justin was swinging. The sky was clear, and the sun was shining. It was a peaceful day, with no chaos happening in the city. Aaron and Sunshine walked out of the front door, and sat next to Justin on the swing. Aaron and Sunshine hugged Justin on the swing. Justin, Aaron, and Sunshine smiled at each other. Justin was swinging with Aaron and Sunshine, enjoying the peaceful nature. Birds were tweeting, and the bugs were buzzing! Aaron tickled Justin on the swing! Justin was laughing super hard on the swing. Justin regained his composure, as Sunshine smiled at him. Sunshine said, "This is what being a family is about, having fun and enjoying each other." Justin and Aaron smiled at each other, as they hugged Sunshine.

Josh Zimmer is an crazy individual with an extreme imagination. He loves to have fun by listening to music, writing stories, and playing video games of various genres such as platforming, multiplayer online games, role playing games, and sports games. His favorite technology brands are Nintendo and Microsoft. They are wonderful role models for the industry. He commands an army of cats to his will with hugs, love, and snacks. He makes the cats purr and meow with happiness.

www.ingramcontent.com/pod-product-compliance
Lightning Source LLC
Chambersburg PA
CBHW071015120726
47910CB00004B/1533